Everyday Machines

Julie Haydon

Contents

NELSON
CENGAGE Learning

Australia • Brazil • Japan • Korea • Mexico • Singapore • Spain • United Kingdom • United States

I use machines every day.
Machines help me do things.

2

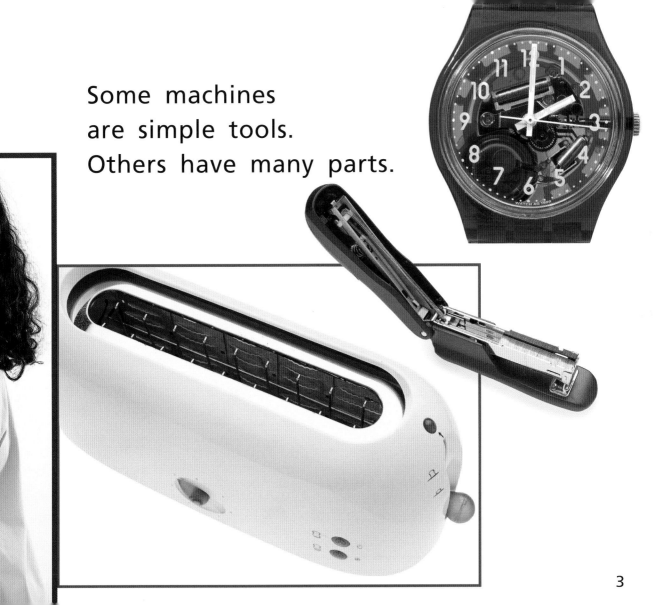

Some machines
are simple tools.
Others have many parts.

3

Home

It is morning.
I wake up
and look at the **clock**.
It is 7 o'clock.
I get up!

Machine:
Clock

Use:
To show
the time

It is time
for breakfast.
I take the cold milk
from the **fridge**.

Machine: Fridge

Use:
To keep food
and drink cold,
so they last longer

5

Then I watch **television**.
I laugh
at the cartoons.

Machine:
Television

Use:
To show a moving picture, so we can learn and have fun

Out and About

I go to the shops with Dad.
We take the car.

Machine:
Car

Use:
To take people from place to place

We buy some flowers
at the shop.
The **cash register**
shows how much
we have to pay.

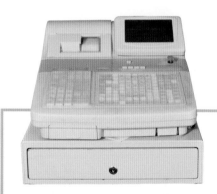

Machine:
Cash register

Use:
To add up
and record
a sale

Dad and I go
to the library.
I look up books
on the **computer**.
Now I can find them
in the library.

Machine:
Computer
Use:
To store
and give us
information

Home Again

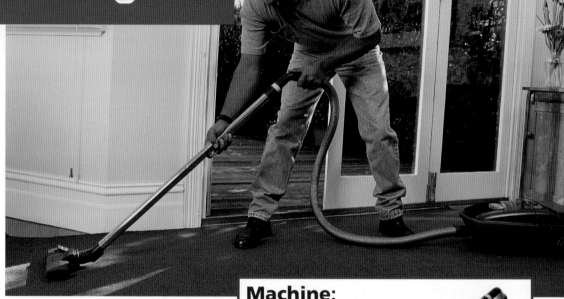

At home, Dad cleans
the floor.
He uses
the **vacuum cleaner.**

Machine:
Vacuum cleaner

Use:
To clean
the floor

It is time for lunch. We heat some soup in the **microwave.**

Machine:
Microwave

Use:
To cook or heat food quickly

Then the **telephone** rings.
It is Jordan!
Jordan is coming to visit.

Machine:	**Use:**
Telephone	To let us talk to people who are far away

Jordan cannot walk.
He has a **wheelchair**
to move around.
We go to the park.

Machine:	**Use**:
Wheelchair	To help a person to move around

13

Then Dad and I
eat dinner together.
I help Dad stack
the **dishwasher.**

Machine:
Dishwasher

Use:
To clean
dishes

It is time for bed.
I say goodnight.
I turn off my **light**
and go to sleep.

Machine:
Light

Use:
To help us see in the dark

Index

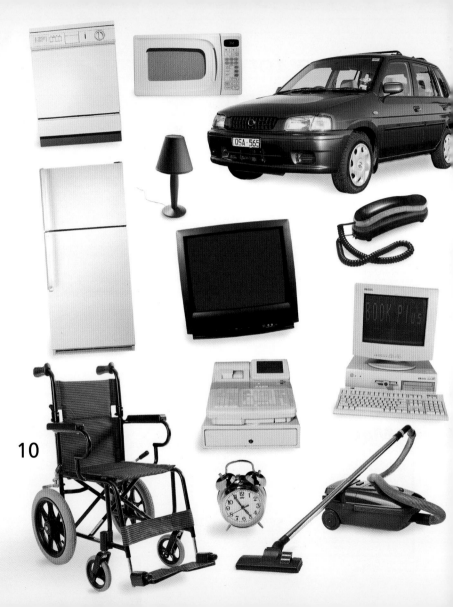